Doc Is the Best Medicine!

By Andrea Posner-Sanchez

Based on the television series created by Chris Nee

Illustrated by Mike Wall

 A GOLDEN BOOK • NEW YORK

ISBN 978-0-7364-3264-1
randomhouse.com/kids
Printed in the United States of America
10 9 8 7 6 5 4 3 2 1

Roll Call

Get to know Doc McStuffins and her friends and family.

Doc McStuffins

Doc is a six-year-old girl who doesn't only play with her toys—she heals them! Doc runs a special doctor's office just for toys. She's great at figuring out what's bothering them and how to make them feel better.

Hallie

Doc's assistant, Hallie, always has the proper medical equipment ready for each case. And this toy hippo really knows how to make nervous patients feel relaxed.

Stuffy

Stuffy likes to think of himself as a brave dragon. Unfortunately, he's actually scared of almost everything! Stuffy also tends to fall, trip, and run into stuff—a lot. It's a good thing one of his best friends is a toy doctor!

Lambie

Lambie is Doc's stuffed lamb and her very best friend. Lambie is sweet and caring, offering cuddles to all the nervous toys. She doesn't like getting dirty and loves pretending to be a princess.

Chilly

Chilly the snowman is always worried he's going to melt. Luckily, his friends are there to remind him that he is a stuffed toy and has nothing to be concerned about!

Emmie

Emmie is Doc's best human friend. She lives right next door, so she and Doc play together all the time.

Sir Kirby

Sir Kirby is a toy knight. He is proud, brave, and always ready to rescue a princess in danger.

Boomer

Boomer is a soccer ball. His favorite thing to do is to bounce, bounce, bounce!

Donny

Donny is Doc's younger brother. Like most four-year-olds, he sometimes breaks his toys by accident. Luckily, his sister can fix them!

Mom

Doc's mother is a doctor, too! Doc has learned a lot from her mom—that's why she's such a good toy doctor!

Dad

Doc's father is a chef. He makes delicious healthy meals for his family.

Disney

DOC McStuffins

A Knight in Sticky Armor

Based on the script "Knight Time" by Sascha Paladino
Illustrated by Mike Wall

"Hi, everyone," Doc McStuffins says to her toys Lambie, Hallie, and Stuffy. Doc's stethoscope begins to glow—and her toys magically come to life. "Let's play princess," she declares.

Lambie loves playing princess. She pretends to be trapped in a castle. "Oh, save me, brave prince!" she cries.

Stuffy is playing the part of the brave prince. He runs toward the castle to rescue the princess but trips on a crayon and falls down. Luckily, Hallie is there to help Stuffy get up.

"Wouldn't it be perfect if we had a real knight in **shining** armor to save me?" Lambie asks from the top of the castle.

Doc thinks that is a good idea. She remembers that her little brother used to play with a toy knight all the time. "I'll see if we can borrow Donny's knight," Doc says.

"I remember that knight," Lambie tells Stuffy and Hallie. "He was really brave—and shiny."

Hallie and Stuffy are excited when Doc comes back from Donny's room. They want to meet the knight.

Doc sets the toy knight on the floor and brings him to life.

"It is I, Sir Kirby, the bravest knight in all of McStuffins Kingdom," he says with a knightly bow.

Doc and the other toys are surprised when they get a closer look at Sir Kirby. He's rather **dirty**.

"We thought you were going to be a lot . . . shinier," Hallie gently tells the knight.

"Alas, my armor has seen shinier days," Sir Kirby says. "I am still a brave knight." He races to rescue Princess Lambie from the castle—but ends up falling over and getting stuck to the rug.

Doc takes a closer look. "Sir Kirby, you don't seem as knightly as you used to," she tells him. "I think there's something wrong with you."

Sir Kirby agrees. "You may be right, Lady McStuffins. My arms and legs aren't working quite the way they should."

Sir Kirby steps forward . . .
and gets stuck to Doc! "I fear I
cannot be the knight I once was,"
he says sadly.

"You know how you're really great at saving princesses?" Doc asks the knight as she walks over to her doctor's bag. "Well, I'm really great at saving toys. I promise I'm going to figure out what's wrong with you and make you better. The Doc is in!"

First, Doc checks Sir Kirby's heartbeat. His heart sounds great, but the stethoscope gets stuck.

Next, Sir Kirby stands against a wall so Doc can measure his height.

"Now please come over to my doctor's bag so I can check one more thing," Doc tells Sir Kirby.

The toy knight tries to step away from the wall, but he's stuck. Again. "Perhaps I can have a little help here?" he asks.

Stuffy tugs and pulls. Finally, Sir Kirby flies off the wall . . . and gets stuck to the rug again.

Doc lifts Sir Kirby up. "You seem to be sticking to everything," she tells him. "I need to figure out why." She examines the knight from head to toe with her magnifying glass. "It looks like you're covered in grape jelly and pizza cheese," Doc declares.

"Yum!" says Stuffy.

"When was the last time you took a bath?" Doc asks Sir Kirby.

"Uh . . . well, let me see. . . . To tell you the truth, I don't think I've ever taken a bath," the knight admits.

"I have a diagnosis!" Doc announces. "You have Filthy-Icky-Sticky Disease. You're covered with sticky food, and your arms and legs aren't moving well. That means that you, Sir Kirby, are not clean."

Sir Kirby hangs his head in shame. "An unclean knight will never do. I beg you to forgive me, but I shall hand in my armor and go."

"You don't have to stop being a knight," Doc tells him. "We can treat Filthy-Icky-Sticky Disease by giving you a **bath** and getting you squeaky-clean."

Doc and Sir Kirby head to the bathroom, where Doc's mother is waiting to give them a bath. They wash up with soap and rinse with clean water.

Sir Kirby likes the
bubbles.

After drying off, Doc and Sir Kirby go back to the bedroom. Stuffy, Lambie, and Hallie **cheer** for the improved and very clean Sir Kirby.

"Thanks to you, Lady McStuffins, I feel like myself again," the knight tells Doc.

"You're welcome," says Doc. "Your Filthy-Icky-Sticky Disease is cured!"

Doc decides it is time to play princess once again.

Lambie heads back to the top of the castle. "Oh, no! There are scary dragons everywhere!" she cries.

"Fear not—I shall protect you!" says Sir Kirby as he marches toward Stuffy.

The toy dragon roars his fiercest roar, but then notices his reflection in the knight's shiny armor and is scared.

"Ahh! A dragon!" Stuffy runs away.

"Oh, Sir Kirby, you are so brave!" exclaims Lambie.
"All in a day's work for the **cleanest** knight in all of
McStuffins Kingdom!" Sir Kirby declares.

Thanks to Doc McStuffins and a bubbly bath, Sir Kirby
has finally saved the princess.

Fun in the Tub

A bath is important for keeping you clean and germ-free. But bath time can also be fun time! Ask your mom or dad to help you try these ideas next time you get into the tub:

Shaving Cream Designs

Use unscented shaving cream to form super-cool hairstyles, beards, and bikini tops on you or a waterproof doll. Then simply dunk in the tub to wash them away.

Water Races

Place two or more floating toys at one end of the tub. Use a spray bottle to squirt water at the toys, or use your hands to make gentle waves. The first toy to the finish line wins!

Time to Glow

Toss some glow sticks in the tub and turn off the light for a fun disco bath!

Toy Spa Day

Sir Kirby loves getting all cleaned up. Ask your parents if you can treat one of your toys to a super-cool spa day. Just make sure the toy won't get damaged if wet!

You can bathe your toy inside or outside. Have an adult fill a bowl or plastic container with a little water. Add some dishwashing liquid to make it a bubble bath!

Put a few drops of dishwashing liquid on a washcloth and gently clean your toy. Use a spray bottle to rinse it off, or wet a second washcloth to wipe the soap off.

Let your toy relax in the tub. You can read it a story or play some soothing music as it soaks.

Dry your toy well with a fluffy towel.

Boomer Gets His Bounce Back

Based on the script "Busted Boomer" by Kent Redeker
Illustrated by Mike Wall

Doc and her friend Emmie are playing soccer. Doc pretends to be a sports announcer. "World-famous soccer star Emmie lines up for the kick. She shoots. . . . She scores!"

Emmie jumps up and down, celebrating her goal. She gives the ball to Doc. "Hmm, the ball felt a little **squishy** when I kicked it," she tells Doc.

"Really? Let me try," says Doc.

Doc kicks the ball. It flies through the air, but it lands with a weak little bounce and s-l-o-w-l-y rolls into the net.

"Way to go, Doc!" shouts Emmie. "You scored a goal!"

But Doc doesn't celebrate. She checks the ball. It is squishier than it should be. "You're right, Emmie," Doc tells her friend. "Something *is* wrong with the ball."

"But we can't stop playing now," says Emmie. "The next kick is for the world championship!"

Doc pretends to be an announcer again.

"Emmie, the best player in the universe, steps up to the ball. Nothing can stop her!"

Emmie gives the ball a **BIG** kick. But it barely moves. It wobbles and rolls and then stops. It doesn't even reach the net!

Emmie picks up the ball and holds it to her ear. She hears a hissing sound.

"I think it has a leak," Emmie says. "You're the best toy fixer there is, Doc. Can you fix it?"

"I'm pretty sure I can," Doc tells Emmie. "And when I get back, we can finish our championship soccer match."

hissss

Doc goes to her clinic and sets the ball down on the check-up table.
She puts on her magic stethoscope. It glows—and all the toys in the
room come to life!

"Hi, guys! I'm Boomer," the ball announces.

"I know you! You're the best bouncing ball I've ever seen!" says Stuffy.

"I love to bounce," Boomer tells all the toys, "but I'm not feeling so bouncy today."

Boomer leaps off the table and lands on the ground with a THUD.

"I should bounce back into the air with a BOING," Boomer says with a sigh. "Why can't I bounce, Doc?"

"I'd like to give you a check-up to see what's going on,"
Doc tells the ball.

Boomer is nervous. "Ooh. A check-up? Uh . . . now that I think
about it, I don't need to bounce."

"You're not scared, are you?" Lambie asks gently.

"No way! I don't get scared. I'm totally not scared," Boomer insists.

"So you'll let me give you a check-up?" Doc asks.

"I guess so." Boomer sighs.

Doc begins the check-up by listening to Boomer's heart
with her stethoscope. "Your heart sounds okay," she reports.

Next, she looks at Boomer's throat with her otoscope.
"Your throat looks fine, too."

When Doc asks Hallie for her next tool, Boomer pulls away and cries, "No, you don't need that!"

"Don't worry. I just need the cuff to check your pressure," Doc tells Boomer as Hallie hands it to her.

"Oh, that. Yeah, go for it," says Boomer, relaxing a bit.

"Hmm . . . Boomer, your pressure is way, way, way down." Doc thinks for a moment and then announces, "Hallie, I have a diagnosis!"

Hallie grabs the *Big Book of Boo-Boos* from the shelf and brings it to Doc.

"Boomer, you have a severe case of Deflate-ulosis!" Doc tells her patient.

Boomer gulps.

"What is that?" asks Lambie.

"Everyone has things that belong on their insides," Doc explains. "Stuffy, Lambie, and Chilly have stuffing. But, Boomer, you're a bouncy ball. You need to be full of air to bounce right."

Doc reaches into her doctor bag. "The first thing I need to do to cure Deflate-ulosis is patch your leak."

Boomer holds still as Doc covers the hole with a patch. "Thanks, Doc! Now I'm ready to go back and play!" Boomer says.

"Not yet," says Doc. "I still have to put more air back inside you."

"Naw, that's all right. I'm good," Boomer claims as he tries to roll away.

Doc thinks she knows why Boomer is scared. "Have you been filled with air before?" she asks the ball.

Boomer nods.

"And you know I'm going to use an air pump?" Doc asks as she pulls a pump from her doctor bag.

"And it has a needle," Boomer says with a sigh. "I'm scared of needles!"

Doc explains that she has to use the needle—it's the only way to fill Boomer back up. Chilly jumps in front of Doc. "Oh, no! I think I need more air inside me, too!" he claims.

"Chilly, you're not a ball," Doc reminds him. Then she turns back to Boomer. But he's gone!

Doc and the toys look all over for Boomer. Finally, Lambie finds the ball hiding inside the dollhouse. "I think you need a cuddle," she tells him as she gives him a big hug.

Doc kneels next to Boomer. "Want to know a secret? When I need to get a shot with a needle from *my* doctor, I'm always scared," she admits. "But my mom comes and gives me a big hug, and that helps me to be brave."

"I like hugs," says Boomer.

"We could *all* give you a hug!" suggests Lambie.

"That should help you feel brave," Doc says.

Hallie, Lambie, Chilly, and Stuffy give Boomer a big hug. Boomer says he feels better already. "Let's do this!"

Doc inserts the needle and starts pumping. "You're being really, really brave!" she tells Boomer.

Boomer starts to get **bigger** as he is filled with more air. "I can feel myself getting bouncier and bouncier!" he shouts.

"Now you should be back to your bold, bouncy self!" Doc declares.
"Thanks for the cuddles," Boomer tells the toys, "but can you un-hug me now? This ball can't wait to bounce!"

Boomer bounces high into the air. He bounces off the dollhouse. He bounces right over Doc and the toys!

"Thank you, Doc!" Boomer yells as he continues bouncing. "I don't know if you knew this, but I *love* bouncing!"

"Aren't you glad you were brave?" asks Stuffy.

"I sure am," admits Boomer. "A few seconds of being brave and now I'm back to bouncing way, way, way high! This is great!"

Doc giggles. "It's great to have you back in bouncing shape," she tells the happy ball. "Now let's go meet up with Emmie so we can finish our world championship soccer match!"

Ready, Set, Move!

Doc and Emmie know that kicking a soccer ball is more than just fun—it's good for them. Any time you're up and moving, you're exercising. And exercising is a great way to stay healthy!

Here are some fun, simple ways to keep moving with your parents and friends:

Do jumping jacks

Ride a bike or a scooter

Jump rope

Play Duck, Duck, Goose

Fly a kite

Have a game of catch

Play tag

Hop like a frog

Walk like a crab

Go for a hike

Doc's Tips

Always wear a helmet when riding a bike, or a scooter, or when skating!
Drink water during and after exercising!

Doc's Tools

A lot of Doc's medical tools are just like the ones your doctor might use during your check-ups. See if you recognize any of them.

Doctor's Bag

Doc has a nice purple and pink doctor's bag. It's the perfect thing to carry her medical tools in when she goes on a house call.

Otoscope

An otoscope has a lens to look through and a light that shines. Doc uses it to examine Boomer's throat. Your doctor may use one to look in your ears and your mouth.

Stethoscope

A doctor uses a stethoscope to listen to your heartbeat and breathing. Doc's stethoscope is magical. When it glows, all her toys come to life!

Magnifying Glass

A magnifying glass makes little things look bigger so they are easier to see. Doc uses one to look closely at the stains on Sir Kirby.

Ruler

Doc uses a ruler to see how tall Sir Kirby is. What does your doctor use to measure you?